Have You Ever Met a Moon Sprite?

PAGE PUBLISHING, INC.
New York, NY

First originally published by Page Publishing, Inc. 2019

ISBN 978-1-64544-000-0 (Paperback)
ISBN 978-1-64424-281-0 (Hardcover)
ISBN 978-1-64424-282-7 (Digital)

Printed in the United States of America

Have You Ever Met a Moon Sprite?

Linda Acton

This book is written, from my heart, for all those who call me Nana! It is about friendship, trust, hope and love! About how being different is good and that everyone is special in their own way! So to all that read this, I hope you enjoy the story, and I hope your lives are full of goodness and happiness and love!

Part One

Meet Isabelle

Back years ago, on a beautiful island of green hills and magical woods lived a young lady named Isabelle. Now Isabelle lived in a small cottage next to the magical woods of the fairies, tiny people with shimmering wings that care for everything in nature. But we will get to them later. Back to Isabelle!

Isabelle, a small woman with bouncy black hair and sparkling brown eyes, was a beauty with a heart of gold! She lived in her cottage by the woods, but she was never bored and never lonely. She had flowers in the yard, a garden in the back, and a brook that ran out of the woods and past her house. And she was a friend to all the creatures in the land. When Isabelle would tend to the flowers and the garden, she would sing the most cheerful songs because they just love to hear her sing. They would grow tall and strong. And she would have the most beautiful flowers and the sweetest fruit and the tastiest vegetables.

4

There were a few animals that lived at the cottage or in the barn. There was a cat named May, who drank milk every morning. Burke, the dog, chased his tail all day. There was Micah, the horse, Jersey, the cow, and Nanny, the goat! They all helped Isabelle in some way around the farm and kept her company. They were her friends, and they all worked together to keep the land nice and neat.

Working around the cottage was fun, and they all enjoyed doing it. For anything you enjoy doing is fun and not like work at all. And when you have help from your friends, well, it just makes it better.

In the mornings after breakfast, Isabelle and May would clean inside the cottage—sweeping and dusting, mopping and shining. Then she would work with Burke in sweeping the porch and cleaning the windows. Clean windows were very important so the sunshine could see in, and Isabelle could see out. She loved to look at the flowers every morning as she ate breakfast.

At noon, Isabelle and Nanny would tend to the yard while Jersey and Micah would clean the barn. Now I bet you're wondering how a cow and a horse could clean a barn? Well, if you really put your mind to it, you can do anything! So yes, a cow and a horse can rake out a barn and pitch the hay! Those jobs were done fairly quickly, and then they all would stop to have lunch.

Early afternoon, Isabelle would tend to the garden and the flowers. This was her most favorite of the jobs around the cottage. And after that was done, the rest of the day was just for fun! She would dance in the field by the brook, and the warm breezes would blow, and the tall, soft grass would sway as if to dance along. Or she would go visit the wood fairies.

In the evenings, as the sun was heading in for the night, Isabelle would sit by the side of the brook and watch the fish play in the water. When the moon would come up, she would lie back and look up at the stars, wondering if anyone lives on them. She would wonder if anyone lived up there, what their lives were like. Did they have babbling brooks and fish? Did they dance in the fields and sing to the flowers? Did they have flowers way up there on the stars?

Then one night, while gazing up at the night sky, trying to imagine what a space flower would look like, she saw a shooting star. Quickly, she made a wish. "I wish," said Isabelle, "I wish I could meet a person from the stars, someone who could tell me if there are flowers up there."

Isabelle didn't know it at the time, but her wish was going to be granted! And soon a new visitor was going to change the lives of Isabelle and all the fairies of the magic woods!

Part Two

The Light from the Sky

As Isabelle walked towards the cottage, ready to turn in for the night, she took one last look at the stars. And to her surprise, she saw another shooting star. Or at least she thought it was at first. But as she watched it, it got closer and brighter. It wasn't a shooting star at all, but what could it be? She watched it closely as it fell closer and closer to the ground. And then with a thud and a bright flash, it landed near the top of the hill behind the barn.

Isabelle ran to the barn and grabbed a lantern, and up the hill she went. As she got closer to where she saw the light landed, she stopped, took a deep breath, and walked slowly towards the glow. She wondered what it could be. Where did it come from? She stopped at the edge of the glow and knelt down to see, and, boy, was she surprised at what she saw!

It looked like a fairy, a fairy from the woods but different at the same time. It was small like the fairies, had wings like the fairies. But it had no hair. Its skin was the color of the lilacs, and its wings sparkled with tiny stars! It had only four fingers and four toes. It was very clear to Isabelle that this wasn't a fairy from the woods. But what was it, and where did it fall from? Isabelle gently scooped it up and wrapped it in her scarf and hurried back to the cottage.

She placed some cotton batting in a small basket and carefully laid the little visitor down and covered it to keep it warm. As she sat in the chair watching it, she hoped that it wasn't hurt in the fall, and that it would be okay. She sat there most of the night watching it, wondering what it would do when it woke up. Finally, she got so sleepy and went on to bed. She's hoping she would have a new friend in the morning.

The next morning when Isabelle woke up, she quickly dressed and made her bed and rushed into the other room to check on her new found friend. But the little visitor was still asleep. Not wanting to wake it, Isabelle quietly made breakfast and told May to be extra quiet as they cleaned. Every now and then, they peeked into the basket just to make sure that it was still there.

They were just finishing up with the cleaning when they heard a small, little sound from the basket. Isabelle quickly put away the last dish and hurried over to the basket and peeked over the edge. The visitor was waking up! With its eyes still closed and its arms stretched up, it gave a big yawn. After a moment, it finally opened its eyes and looked around. Then it saw Isabelle and May peeking over the edge of the basket. Startled, it quickly pulled the cover up over its head. Isabelle realized that it was frightened and stepped back a bit from the basket. In a very soft voice, she whispered, "I think we frightened the poor little thing, May. Why don't you go out on the porch 'til I can get it to eat something?" And out the door May went.

"Please, don't be afraid, little one," said Isabelle. "We are all friends here. Please come out so I know you're okay and not hurt from your fall." The little visitor popped its head out from under the covers and quickly asked, "What fall? Where am I, and who are you? How did I get here, and what was that creature you sent away?"

"Slow down," Isabelle laughed. "My name is Isabelle, and you are in my home. That creature is May, my cat. She lives here with me along with some other friends. You fell from the sky last night and landed on the hill behind the barn. Were you hurt in the fall? Where did you come from?"

The little visitor stood up and bounced once or twice, stretched its arms, and flittered its wings. Then looked up at Isabelle and said, "No, I'm okay. The last thing I remember, I was sweeping a pile of moondust. I must have gotten too close to the edge of the moon and fell off."

"Are you a fairy?" Isabelle asked. "You sort of look like the wood fairies but different."

"I'm a moon sprite," the visitor said. "My name is Titari. What is a fairy? Are they friendly?"

"Oh yes," said Isabelle. "We are all friends here. A fairy is a little person sort of like you. They take care of all things in nature. After you eat, we can go meet all my friends. They will be excited to meet a new friend."

Part Three

18

Out to Meet New Friends

After Isabelle fixed Titari something to eat, they headed out into the yard. "Everything is so much different here than it is on the moon," Titari told Isabelle. "Your ground is so green and fuzzy here." Isabelle giggled. "This is grass," she said. "It tickles your feet when you walk in it barefoot. Come, meet my friends. They are all in the back by the garden. And then we will go to the woods so you can meet the fairies."

Isabelle introduced all her animal friends to Titari. "This is May, the cat. You saw her in the cottage. And there is Burke. He's a dog. Micah is a horse, Jersey is a cow, and that's Nanny, the goat. We all live here at the cottage and take care of it and the gardens. Friends, this is Titari. She is a moon sprite. She fell off the moon last night and landed on the hill." The animals came up to see the new visitor and welcomed her. All but Nanny—you know how stubborn a goat can be. "Nanny," said Isabelle, "come greet our new friend." Nanny just stood there looking at Titari, unwilling to say hi. "Nanny," Isabelle said again, "we are all friends here, and Titari would like to be your friend too."

Titari, realizing that Nanny was just a little unsure because of how different she looked, flew up and patted Nanny on the head. "I am very pleased to meet you, Nanny, and I'm sure we will be the best of friends." Nanny, realizing that just because someone looks, acts, or talks different doesn't mean they all can't be friends, she finally welcomed Titari to the cottage. And then Titari pulled a small star out from her pocket and placed it on Nanny's head. "This will keep us close even when we are apart. And we will be best friends always." Nanny gave Titari a little nudge with her nose to say thank you, and they all walked around the yard showing Titari everything.

Isabelle told Titari all about the vegetables in the garden, the fruits in the trees, and how sweet the apples and melons were. And that the green beans were her favorite. She told her how working in the garden was her favorite job of all.

Isabelle told Titari all about the flowers and the plants there at the cottage. She told her how she sang to the flowers and danced in the fields. And how she sat at the brook in the evenings to watch the fish play. And how she would lie on the grass and watch the stars, wondering what was up there. Then she told Titari how she made a wish on a shooting star and how it might have come true. How else did Titari come to fall right on that hill?

Titari told Isabelle about the flowers and the trees on the moon, and that she too lived alone. Everyone else stayed in the dark. They thought the light from the sun would burn them. But Titari loved the sun, so she lived in the light. She didn't have any friends to be with her and keep her company, so she just kept busy sweeping up the moondust. But she never knew what to do with it, so she just swept it right off the edge of the moon.

"Oh dear," said Isabelle, "I could never imagine living my whole life in the dark or being without my friends. But you will never be alone here. You can stay at the cottage with me. I'm sure you will be happy here. You will have so many friends, and you won't have to sweep anymore dust unless you want to. There are so many fun things to do here. I just know you will find something that fits you just right."

"My word, this is all so exciting," said Titari. "I could just fly all the way to Jupiter and back! I don't know what I want to do first. I want to meet everyone and try everything."

"Hold on, little one," Isabelle said as she laughed at Titari's excitement. "Before you go blasting off to space with joy, why don't we all get some lunch? Then we can head off to the magical woods."

Isabelle took Micah, Jersey, and Nanny to the barn and got them some fresh oats. At the cottage, she got Burke a nice bone and May a bit of tuna. Then she and Titari sat at the table for some chicken salad and ice tea. They had a very nice lunch together.

Part Four

Titari Meets Feather

After lunch, Isabelle and Titari started out for the magical woods. Isabelle was hoping that the fairies would be out and about so she could introduce them to her new friend. As they wandered around the woods, Titari was fascinated with all the different trees and plants there were. "On the moon," she told Isabelle, "we don't have anything like the woods. We have trees and plants but not like this and not so many in one place."

Suddenly, up ahead, they heard a little voice. "Come on, Titari," said Isabelle. "That sounds like Feather. She takes care of all the birds here in the woods." When they got to Feather, she was up by a tree branch and seemed to be deep in thought. She was flying back and forth, tapping her chin with her finger and mumbling to herself.

"Hello, Feather," said Isabelle. "I would like you to meet my new friend."

"Oh hello, Isabelle, did you say something?" Feather asked. "Yes, I did," said Isabelle. "I want you to meet my new friend." Feather looked down on the ground around Isabelle and around the bottom of the tree. Then she looked back at Isabelle and asked, "Who are you talking about. I don't see anyone?" Isabelle laughed and said, "Look behind you, silly. She is up there with you." Feather turned around, looked at Titari for a second, and slowly flew down to Isabelle. "Why does she look like that?" whispered Feather. "This is Titari. She's not a fairy like you are, Feather," Isabelle said. "She's a moon sprite. She is from the moon."

"Oh," said Feather. "How do you do?" And back to mumbling she went.

"You seem to have something troubling you," Titari said to Feather. "Is there anything we can help you with?"

"I am troubled," said Feather. "There is a bird caught in the vines in that thicket there, and it is too dark in there for me to see to get him out."

"Have you tried to call the light fairy?" asked Isabelle. "I tried," said Feather. "But she is in the woods on the other side of the island and won't be back 'til tomorrow. I just don't know what to do. He can't stay tangled in those vines all night."

"Maybe we can use a lantern to help you see in there," Isabelle suggested. "Oh no," said Feather. "It might start a fire in the thicket, and that would be bad."

"Yes, I suppose you're right," Isabelle answered. "And we don't want that to happen. That will be very bad indeed."

"Maybe I can help," said Titari. "Maybe there is something I can do to help get the poor little bird from the vines."

"I don't know," said Feather. "What do you know about birds or vines or thickets? I just don't see how you could help. Oh dear, what will I do?"

"It's true, on the moon where I came from, we don't have birds or vines or thickets," said Titari. "But I do know about the dark, and I am sure, if you give me a chance, that together we can have that bird out in a wink. Won't you please let me help you?"

"Okay," said Feather. "I have to try something. Let's go, and we will see what you can do." And down to the thicket they both flew.

Once there, Titari stepped just inside the thicket and pulled her wings around her as if she was cold. Then with just a whisper, the stars on her wings began to glow. With a smile, her wings lit up so bright that all the dark inside the thicket was gone. "Oh my," said Feather. "Even the light fairy would be surprised at a light that bright." And with that said, Feather went to work carefully untangling the bird from the vines. And quick as a wink, he was free, and he hopped out of the thicket and flew up to the nearest tree branch.

"Thank you," Feather said to Titari, "for all your help. And please forgive me for being so rude to you. I have never seen wings like that before. They are truly amazing. I am very glad to meet you and would like to welcome you to the magical woods."

"Thank you," Titari said. "And I would like to give you a gift. Take this small moonstone. And if you ever find yourself in a dark spot again, just hold it in your hand and whisper. It will give you all the light you need." And she handed Feather the moonstone.

"Oh my. Isabelle, look," said Feather. "Look at this, my very own moonstone. Wait 'til the others see this. Thank you, Titari, thank you oh so much." And with that said, Feather was off on her way. Isabelle and

Titari smiled at each other and waved to the little bird, and then went on their way to find more fairies for Titari to meet. "That was very nice of you to help Feather, and she truly loved the gift," Isabelle said as she walked along. Titari just smiled.

Part Five

Dew Drops by the Brook

As they wandered along through the woods, Isabelle could hear the water in the brook. "Let's go to the brook," Isabelle told Titari. "I bet we will find Dew Drop there. She takes care of all the fish and the water in the woods."

"That will be great to see," Titari said. "There is so little water on the moon." So down to the brook they went.

When they got to the brook, they both took off their shoes and stuck their feet in the water. "This feels so nice," Titari said. "I have never had water flow between my toes before, and it is so warm." Just then someone called from down the brook. It was Dew Drop. "Isabelle, Isabelle, come quick! I need your help!" Isabelle and Titari grabbed their shoes and hurried to help Dew Drop. "Isabelle," Dew Drop said a bit out of breath. "This rock has fallen on the fish, and he can't get his tail out. Can you help me please and move the rock?"

"Of course I will," Isabelle said.

Isabelle lifted the rock and set it aside where it wouldn't fall in the water again. "Oh my, oh my," cried Dew Drop. "The rock has broken the poor little fish's tail. How will he be able to swim with his tail broke? This is not good, not good at all. How do you fix a fish tail? You can't just put a Band-Aid on it, what…?" And Dew Drop stopped talking. She had looked up at Isabelle and saw Titari sitting on her shoulder.

"Oh, I didn't know you were not alone," said Dew Drop. "It's okay," said Isabelle. "This is Titari. She is my new friend from the moon. She is a moon sprite, and I have brought her to meet all the fairies."

"Oh," Dew Drop said again. "Well, I have no time for visiting. I have to find a way to fix the tail on this poor little fish. Can you help me find a way?"

"I will do what I can," said Isabelle.

"Perhaps I could be of some help," Titari offered. "Would you let me try to help the fish?"

"I don't know," said Dew Drop. "You don't even have webbed feet like me. What could you possibly know about water creatures? I guess, 'til I figure out a way, you can try as long as you don't make it any worse."

"I will try my best," Titari promised and sat on the edge of the brook where the little fish was waiting for someone to help him. "Don't worry, my little friend. I think I know just what to do," Titari told the fish. And she reached into her pouch and pulled out a tiny little star. Holding it up in front of her, she said a little whisper and tapped the top of it, then a small, glittering tail started growing from the bottom of it. When it got big enough to cover the little fish's tail, Titari said, "That will do for now." And the stars tail stopped growing.

"What is that?" Dew Drop asked with a very surprised look on her face. "This," said Titari, "is a shooting star. And everyone knows that shooting stars have tails." With that, Titari took the tail off the star and leaned down to the little fish. "This won't hurt a bit, little friend," she said as she placed the star tail on the hurt tail of the fish. And magically the star tail clung to the hurt tail of the fish and began to sparkle, just like the night stars do. And in a matter of seconds, the little fish was swimming better than ever.

"My, my, my," said Dew Drop, "that was the most amazing thing I have ever seen, ever. Would you please accept my apology for ever doubting you?"

"No problem," Titari said as she flew up next to Dew Drop. "I was glad to help. And I am very pleased to meet you."

"I am so glad that Isabelle brought you to the woods today," said Dew Drop. "And I am sure that we will be very good friends. Welcome, welcome to the woods."

Titari looked down at the little fish and gave him a wink before he swam off down the brook. "I would like you to have this," she told Dew Drop and handed her the tiny star. "You never know when you may need the magic tail again. Just hold it up, say a little whisper, and tap the top, and the tail will grow. When you think you have enough, just say, 'That will do for now.' It is a very useful thing to have."

"My, my, my," said Dew Drop, "my very own shooting star! Thank you so much. I will take very good care of it. I can't wait to show the other fairies." And off she went. Isabelle and Titari went on their way too, hoping to meet a few more fairies before they had to head back to the cottage for the night. "Let's go towards the flower field in the middle of the woods and see who we find there," said Isabelle.

Part Six

Petal's New Flower

When Isabelle and Titari first reached the flower field, they didn't see anyone. But as they neared the middle, they saw Petal, fluttering from flower to flower.

"Hello, Petal," Isabelle yelled as she walked through the field.

"Well, hello, Isabelle," Petal yelled back. "What brings you to the woods today?"

"I brought my new friend to meet all the fairies," Isabelle replied.

"I would love to," Petal replied. "And where is your new friend?" Just then Titari flew up from a bunch of tulips where she was enjoying the scent and said, "Hello."

"Oh," Petal gasped. "Where did you come from?"

"This is Titari," Isabelle told her. "She fell from the moon last night and landed behind my barn. She is a moon sprite and my new friend."

"She must have landed in a patch of lilacs," Petal said. "And their color rubbed off on her."

"No, I'm supposed to be this color," Titari said. "All moon sprites are this color."

"Oh," Petal said again. "Well, I am very pleased to meet you, but I don't have time to chat right now. I have to get back to my search."

"Is there something we can do to help you, Petal?" asked Isabelle.

"I got a special request from the Queen herself," Petal said excitedly. "And I really don't want to let her down. She has a patch of ground by her castle and would like to plant some flowers there. But the sun cannot shine in this patch, so she wants flowers that will grow without sunshine. So far, all my flowers need at least a little sunshine to grow. I just don't know what I am going to tell her. She is so looking forward to having new flowers there. I must be on my way and keep looking." And Petal turned to continue her search.

"What kind of flowers grow without sunshine? I wonder," Isabelle said looking around the clearing. "I know," said Titari. "Let's catch up with Petal. I think I can help end her search." And off they went after Petal.

"Petal," called Titari, "I think I can help you with your flower. I know of one that grows without sunshine." Petal stopped and turned to Titari. "You?" she asked with surprise in her voice. "You are from the moon. What do you know about the flowers here?" Titari smiled and replied, "Only that they smell sweet. But if you could please show me this patch where the sun won't shine." Petal looked at Isabelle, and Isabelle nodded her head. "Give her a chance, Petal," Isabelle said. "You may be very surprised."

"I am in such a spot right now," said Petal. "I am willing to try anything." So off they went.

When they reached the castle of the fairy queen, Petal showed them a place under a rock ledge that the sunshine could not reach. "This is it," she replied. "It is such a gloomy spot in all this beauty, and I just don't know what to plant here. There are no flowers in the woods that will grow without any sunshine at all."

"If I may," said Titari, "I do have a solution that will brighten this spot. I don't know about the flowers here, but I do know about the ones on the moon." Then she pulled some strange tiny seeds from her pouch. They were light green, and they glowed in the dark. Titari planted the seeds and said a little whisper and up popped some little sprouts. Petal and Isabelle were amazed at how fast they grew. And in just a few minutes, the sprouts bloomed into the most beautiful flowers. They were green with six petals and glowed like the moon on a clear night.

"How beautiful," Petal said. "I have never seen a flower like that before. Is that a moon flower?"

"It is," replied Titari. "It will bloom every day without sunshine, and it will grow forever."

"Thank you oh so much," Petal said as she gave Titari a little hug. "The queen will be so pleased. I do wish she were here to meet you now."

"That's okay," Titari said. "I am sure to meet her soon."

Titari then reach into her pouch again and pulled out a tiny, dry flower bud on a stem and handed it to Petal. "I would like you to have this," she told Petal. "Just say a little whisper, and it will give you moon flower seeds to plant anywhere you need them."

"Oh, thank you," Petal told Titari. "Thank you very much. I'm very glad I met you today. You have been such a big help to me. I'm going to show this to all my friends." And off she flew.

Part Seven

Hopper Needs a Hand

"It's getting close to supper time I think," said Isabelle. "Maybe we should head back towards the cottage. We may still see a fairy or two on the way back. And we can come back tomorrow so you can meet the others."

"I have made so many new friends today," Titari told Isabelle. "I am so glad you wished on that star." And on through the woods they went.

Isabelle walked through the woods with Titari sitting on her shoulder. She had walked for about ten minutes and was beginning to think that they wouldn't see any more fairies today. Suddenly, they heard a commotion coming from behind a large tree. As they rounded the tree, they saw Hopper trying to gather up ten little frogs. "Hopper takes care of all the critters that go on land and in the water," Isabelle told Titari.

"What are you doing, Hopper?" Isabelle asked. "Hi, Isabelle," Hopper said. "I told Ms. Frog that I would watch her children while she went shopping, and there are so many. I can hardly keep track of them all."

"You do seem to have your hands full," Isabelle laughed. "Is there anything we can do to help?"

"We?" asked Hopper. "Who is with you?"

"My new friend from the moon," Isabelle answered as she looked around to see where Titari had gotten off to. "Oh, there you are. What are you doing, Titari?"

"I wanted to see these little creatures a little closer, and I guess I got a little to close," Titari laughed bouncing on the back of a little frog as it hopped around.

"Well, well, well," said Hopper. "And just what do you think you're doing? Ms. Frog surely won't be happy if anything happened to any of her children."

"I wouldn't hurt any of them," said Titari. "I came down for a look, and it jumped up and caught me. I'm sorry if I alarmed you."

"Well, just be more careful next time," Hopper said. And he went back to chasing the little frogs, trying to keep them all together. "I do believe those little frogs are getting the best of you, Hopper," Isabelle laughed. "Are you sure we can't do anything to help?"

"Well," Hopper replied, "do you have a playpen that we could put these little jumpers in?" Isabelle patted the pockets of her dress and sadly replied, "No. I'm afraid I don't. But maybe Titari will have something that will help."

"I do believe," Titari answered. "I just might. Yes, indeed I do." And she pulled a silver ring out of her pouch. "And just how, may I ask, is that little ring going to help keep all ten of these little frogs together?" asked Hopper. "You can't even fit one frog in that. That's not going to help me any."

"Just wait, Hopper," Isabelle told him. "Give Titari a chance. I bet she will amaze you."

"Well, all right," said Hopper. "But if anything goes wrong, you have to tell Ms. Frog."

"Don't worry," said Titari. "It will be just fine."

Titari flew down by the little frogs and gathered them all together. "Watch closely," she told them as she flew just above their heads. Holding the silver ring out in front of her, she said a little whisper. To everyone's surprise, a ring of light came from the ring and fell all around the little frogs. When it reached the ground, Titari said, "That will do for now."

And the ring in her hand stopped glowing. On the ground, all around the little frogs was a circle of light that kept them all together but gave them room to play.

"Well, well," Hopper said, "that was truly amazing. Please forgive me for being so rude. Where did you say you were from?"

"I came from the moon," Titari told him. "I am a moon sprite."

"Well, I am very pleased to meet you," Hopper said. "And thank you for all your help. I really had my hands full."

"You're very welcome," Titari answered. "And I would like for you to have this ring. It is a silver ring from Saturn. Just give a little whisper, and it will give you a magic ring for whatever you may need. When it's the size you want, just say, 'That will do for now,' and it will stop growing. When you no longer need the ring, just say, 'Job done,' and it will disappear."

"Well, well, well," replied Hopper, "I don't know what to say. Thank you. Thank you oh so much. When Ms. Frog returns for her children, I'm going to rush home and show everyone the special gift I got from my new friend from the moon."

"We must be going," Isabelle said. "It is almost time to eat. We will be coming back to the woods tomorrow. There are a few more fairies that Titari hasn't met yet."

"I hope to see you again," Titari hollered as they went on their way.

Back at the cottage, Isabelle and Titari sat down for a nice meal of potato soup and barley bread. Then off to bed they went. Tomorrow would surely be another adventure for them both.

Part Eight

A Sweet Treat for Maze

The next morning, Isabelle and Titari ate breakfast and got all the cleaning and chores done early. They packed them a picnic lunch and headed off to the woods. Titari was excited and hoping to meet the other fairies. They followed the brook into the woods this time so they could enjoy their picnic by the water later. On the way, they saw the little fish they helped the day before swimming with his fancy new tail. They waved, and he gave them a little splash to say hi.

After a while, they came to a spot in the woods where there were more trees and the ground stayed damp. "We should go another way," said Isabelle. "We don't want to picnic on the wet ground." Just then Maze called out to Isabelle. "Hi, Isabelle. What brings you out to the woods today?"

"Well, hello, Maze," Isabelle said in return. "I brought my new friend to meet the fairies."

"I love new friends," said Maze as she flew over to Isabelle. But she stopped quickly when she saw Titari sitting on her shoulder. "I don't want to alarm you, Isabelle," said Maze, "but there is a strange bug on your shoulder. Maybe we can catch it and take it to Bumble. He might know what it is."

"Silly Maze," Isabelle said. "This is not a bug. This is my new friend. Meet Titari. She is a moon sprite." Maze flew up to Titari and looked at her, front and back. "I don't know," said Maze. "She doesn't really look like a bug up close. She has arms and legs and wings like me. But she only has four fingers and toes. She has no hair, and she is the color of the lilacs. Was she born wrong?"

"No, no," Isabelle said. "She was born just right. She is from the moon, and this is the way she is supposed to look."

"Oh," said Maze with a smile, "then I think she looks just fine. How do you do? I am very pleased to meet you. I take care of all the plants in the woods."

"What are you doing out this way?" Isabelle asked. "There are plenty of trees but no plants. I figured if anyone would be here, it would be Willow."

"Well," said Maze, "I came to look around and see if I could get some plants to grow here. But only a little sunshine gets in here, and it is very damp. I don't think I can help this place much. I guess I will just leave it for Willow."

"If I may," said Titari, "have you thought about mushrooms?"

"Yes, I have," Maze answered. "But there are so many mushrooms growing in the woods now. We really don't need any more."

"Then would you consider a different kind of mushroom?" Titari asked. "One like no other you have here."

"We have every kind of mushroom there is in the woods. What other kind could there be?" asked Maze. "Let me show you," said Titari, "here in this spot." And she flew down to a clear spot on the ground.

From her pocket, she pulled a tiny amount of what looked like powder and held it in her hand. She said a little whisper and blew the powder onto the ground. And instantly, tiny little pink mushrooms popped up out of the damp soil. They didn't get very big, but they did grow fast. "That's great," said Maze. "But they are just little pink mushrooms."

"Yes," said Titari. "But taste one."

Maze flew down and picked a mushroom. "It's just a mushroom, right?" she asked. "And it's one you can eat?"

"Yes, you can eat it." Titari told her. "But it is a special mushroom from the moon. Go ahead and try it. I promise it won't hurt you, and you will like it." Maze looked at Isabelle, scrunched her nose, squinted her eyes, and took a bite of the mushroom. Then a big smile came across her face. "Wow," she said with surprise. "I have never had a mushroom like this before. It taste like candy. It's a candy mushroom!" Maze picked a few more and took one to Isabelle as she stuffed a few more in her mouth. "These are delicious," she said stuffing one in Isabelle's mouth. "Thank you, Titari, very much. They are delicious," said Isabelle. "They are very sweet."

"I would like to give you this gift," Titari told Maze, and she pulled a small brush from her pouch. It looked like a tiny broom. "You are giving me a toy broom?" Maze asked her. "No," Titari answered. "It is a magic brush. Just give it a whisper, and it will give you the dust to grow these mushrooms. Whenever I found a wet spot on the moon, I would grow me some for a snack."

"Well, thank you," said Maze. "And I promise to share them with all my friends. I have to go show them right away." And off she went through the woods to find the other fairies.

Titari sat back up on Isabelle's shoulder, and they went on to find them a spot to have their picnic. "Do you think we can have some of those candy mushrooms with our lunch?" Isabelle asked. "They are very good."

"Of course we can," Titari answered. "I have a little more dust in my pocket."

Part Nine

It's Hunny and Bunny

Isabelle and Titari found a nice dry spot by the brook for their picnic and had a very nice lunch. They had just finished cleaning things up when across the brook they heard some arguing. "This way," said one voice. "No, this way," said the other voice. "We didn't lose her, did we?"

"No, we didn't," said the first voice. "We just can't find her." And from across the brook came Hunny and Bunny.

"What are you two arguing about?" asked Isabelle. Hunny and Bunny stopped and looked at Isabelle. "Oh, Isabelle," Hunny said. "It is awful, just awful."

"It's not awful," Bunny replied. "But it may be bad. We lost a baby chipmunk."

"You lost a baby?" asked Titari, popping out from behind the picnic basket. "How did you lose a baby?" Hunny and Bunny looked at each other and flew behind Isabelle. "It's a monster," said Bunny. "A purple monster," said Hunny. "No, no," Isabelle assured them. "It's just my friend Titari. She is from the moon. She's a moon sprite."

"Cool beans," said Hunny. "Yee haw," said Bunny. "Can we be her friend too? I saw her first," said Hunny. "She is my friend."

"No, I saw her first," said Bunny. "She's my friend."

"Wait," said Titari. "I will be friends with both of you."

Hunny and Bunny stopped and clapped their hands with joy. "We have a new friend, a new friend from the moon," they sang out together. They introduced themselves as they curtsied to Titari. "We are sisters," said Hunny. "Twin sisters," said Bunny. "We take care of the animals here in the woods," said Hunny. "But not very well today I'm afraid," said Bunny. "I'm sure it will be okay," said Isabelle. "We will help you. Tell us how you lost the baby chipmunk."

"We were playing hide-and-seek with the baby chipmunk," said Hunny. "It was her turn to hide. We counted to ten like we were supposed to," said Bunny. "But we have been looking and looking, and just can't find her."

"Mother chipmunk is going to be so upset with us. Can you help us look for her?" asked Hunny. "Please," said Bunny. "We have looked everywhere. We don't know what else to do."

"Of course we will," said Isabelle. "The baby couldn't have gone too far. Where did you see her last"

"Just there," said Hunny. "On the other side of the brook," said Bunny. "Okay, then we start there," Isabelle told them. And they all crossed the brook. "Here," said Hunny. "Right here," said Bunny. "This is where we were counting."

"Okay," said Isabelle. "So which way do we go?"

"I think I can help with that," said Titari. "I have something that just might lead us right to the baby chipmunk." She reached into her pouch and pulled out a crystal. "Is that a magic crystal?" asked Hunny. "Can I touch it?" asked Bunny. "No, this is not a magic crystal," answered Titari, and she reached back into her pouch and pulled out another. "This is a magic crystal," she said as she held the two pieces together.

She held the crystal up above her head and said a little whisper. Suddenly, from up in the sky came a beam of light. Not bright but soft and it shined all the way to the ground. "This way," said Titari as she flew off in the direction the light beam fell. And when they reached the end, it was shining on the trunk of an old tree. "There," said Titari. "That's where you will find the baby." Hunny and Bunny flew up to a hole in the trunk and looked in. "She's here," yelled Hunny. "She's sleeping," whispered Bunny. "We will wait right here 'til she wakes up, and then take her home."

"I would like for you two to have these crystal pieces," Titari told the twins. "I think you need them more than I do." But she told them that they won't work alone. They had to be together. "Just like the two of you," said Isabelle. "You work together."

"Just remember," Titari said, "hold them up together, and say a little whisper. The moonbeam will come down and show you where you need to go."

"Cool beans," said Hunny. "Our very own moon crystal."

"Yee haw," said Bunny. "Wait 'til the other fairies see what we have. I hope the baby chipmunk wakes up soon so we can go show everyone what we have."

"Thank you, Titari," said Hunny. "Thank you very much," said Bunny. "We are so glad to have a new friend."

71

"Yes," said Hunny. "Welcome to the woods."

"Thank you," said Titari. "I am so glad I met both of you. I am sure we will become dear friends." And Titari sat back on Isabelle's shoulder, and off they went. "I hope we get to see the rest of the fairies today," Isabelle said. "I think we should go this way and see who we run into next."

73

Part Ten

Bumble Bounces In

As they walked through the woods, Isabelle sang a cheerful song to pass the time. The sun was shining through the trees, the woods smelled of fresh bloomed flowers, and the butterflies were playing everywhere. "This is a beautiful place to live," Titari said. "There aren't any places like this on the moon. I bet the fairies really love living here."

"Yes, they do," said Isabelle. "The fairies have lived in these woods for many, many years."

Titari flew off of Isabelle's shoulder and was playing with the butterflies. Isabelle smiled and laughed. She was glad to see how happy Titari was. She walked slowly so she could watch Titari playing. Fluttering around with all the butterflies, she was really having a good time. Then suddenly, out of nowhere, *bam!* Something crashed right into Titari. Isabelle ran over and picked Titari up off the ground. "Are you okay?" she asked

Titari. "Yes," said Titari "But what was that? It felt like I was hit by a comet."

"It was me," said a voice from the grass. "I guess I went left when I should have gone right. That was the hardest butterfly I have ever crashed into." Isabelle looked through the grass 'til she found who the voice was coming from. "It's Bumble! He takes care of all the bugs in the woods. Are you okay, Bumble?" Isabelle asked him. "It wasn't a butterfly you ran into. It was Titari."

"What is a Titari?" Bumble asked sitting up and shaking his head. "I am," said Titari, and she flew down to Bumble. "May I help you up since I sort of helped you down?" Titari giggled.

"So you're a Titari, but what are you?" Bumbled asked. "I'm a moon sprite," Titari said, "from the moon. I fell off the edge and landed here. Isabelle saved me. Here, let me help you up. Are your wings okay?"

"Oh yes," said Bumble. "I crash all the time. I was on my way to see a spider friend. Lady bug said that he had a problem and needed my help. That's why I was in a hurry."

"Oh," said Isabelle, "we will go with you. Maybe we can help too. Show us the way, Bumble. We will be right behind you."

"It's not far," Bumble said. "Just up by this tree." Isabelle and Titari followed Bumble up to a large tree. "I'm here," yelled Bumble. "Where are you?"

"Oh, there you are. Lady Bug said you needed my help." Bumble was talking to a spider sitting at the bottom of a tree. "What is the spider saying?" asked Titari. "I don't know," said Isabelle. "I don't speak spider. Is there anything we can do to help?" Isabelle asked Bumble. "I'm not sure," Bumble told her. "This is sort of a strange problem."

"It seems that I'm not the only one that crashes around here," Bumble said. "This poor little spider has fallen out of the tree and broke his spinnerets. Without them, he can't make a web. I can make lightning bugs light and teach ball bugs to roll, but I can't make a spiderweb. How am I going to help the spider? I don't know what to do."

"We will help you think of something," Isabelle told him. "Yes, we will," said Titari. "But what is a spiderweb? We don't have spiders on the moon."

Isabelle looked around for a spiderweb to show Titari. "Oh, here's one," she called to Titari. "This is a spiderweb. They live in it."

"Oh, Bumble," Titari yelled, "I think I can help. We don't have spiders on the moon, but we do have something like the web." Titari went over to where Bumble was sitting with the spider. "I can help him make webs, but he will have to carry a tiny seed with him. Will that be okay?" Titari explained. Bumble told the spider what she said, and then told Titari that the little spider agreed. "I will need your help too, Bumble. I need some way to make the seed stick to the spider."

Bumble got some tree sap on a stick and took it to Titari. Titari pulled a small flower from her pouch, said a little whisper, and out popped three small seeds. "Where would you like your web to be?" she asked the spider. The spider pointed to a spot between two leaves on a plant next to the tree. Titari squeezed one seed, and out popped a web and stuck between the leaves. It was perfect. "Now the glue," Titari asked Bumble. And she put a spot of glue on one seed and put it on the spider's belly. The other she put in the web so the spider would have an extra for later. "All you have to do is squeeze it lightly, and a web will string out. Squeeze hard for a whole web."

"This is for you, Bumble," said Titari, and she gave him the flower. "We call it a starlight bloom on the moon. All you have to do is say a little whisper, and it will give you three seeds. They come in handy for lots of things."

"Oh, thank you," said Bumble. "I can't wait to show everyone what I have." The little spider waved to Titari and curled up in his new web. Bumble took off to show his gift, and Isabelle and Titari went looking for more friends to meet. It had been a great day so far.

Part Eleven

Willow's Picky Tree

Isabelle and Titari went on through the woods laughing about how Bumble went left instead of right and crashed right into Titari. And Titari talked about how much fun she had flying with the butterflies. "I really like it here in the woods," Titari said. "The smell of the flowers, the birds singing. It is so much better than the moon."

"Well, look at that," said Isabelle. "That tree doesn't have any leaves on it. It should be covered with leaves just like all the others. I wonder if Willow knows about this. She takes care of all the trees here in the woods."

"Yes, yes, I know," said Willow as she flew down from the big tree next to it. "This is the pickiest tree I have ever had to work with. It just doesn't like any of the leaves that I try to grow on it."

"How can that be?" asked Isabelle. "Shouldn't it grow leaves just like the other trees?"

"Yes, yes, it should," answered Willow. "But it doesn't want to be like the other trees. It wants to be different."

"I understand different," said Titari as she flew up next to Isabelle. "I understand different very well."

"Yes. You certainly are different," said Willow. "But just who are you?"

"This is Titari," said Isabelle. "She is my friend from the moon. She is a moon sprite."

"Yes, yes, I would say a moon sprite is different here in these woods," said Willow.

"Are there no leaves you can give the tree to make her happy?" Isabelle asked Willow. "I have tried every leaf I know," said Willow. "But she sheds them all. None I have tried has made her happy. I have tried all the tree leaves, flower leaves, and plant leaves and nothing. She just shakes them right off. She insists on being different from all the other things with leaves. I just don't know what else to try."

"I have an idea," said Titari. "If you let me help, I can give her some very special leaves. And I bet she will be very proud of them and keep them on always. Leaves that will make her different from any other tree.

She will be different and not like the others. And I'm sure you will be pleased with the way they look."

"I don't know," said Willow. "She is a very picky tree. I just don't know why she wants to be different."

"But different is good," said Titari. "Not everything can always be the same. You do have different kinds of trees here in the woods. And Petal has many different kinds of flowers. If everything were the same, then the woods wouldn't be this beautiful."

"I guess you're right," Willow said. "Go ahead, and give it a try. If being different makes the tree happy, then it will be okay with me."

Titari reached into her pouch and pulled out a small wand with a star on top. She flew over to the tree, said a little whisper, and tapped the tree with the wand. Tiny little golden sprouts started popping out all over the branches. And before you knew it, they grew into beautiful, golden leaves that looked just like stars. The tree loved her new leaves so much. She stretched out her branches so they could be seen by every tree around.

"Those are the most beautiful leaves I have ever seen on a tree," Isabelle said. "Yes, yes, they are," said Willow. "And she is keeping them on. See how proud she looks. How can I ever thank you for making this tree so happy?"

"I'm just glad I could help," said Titari. "And I would like you to have this star wand. It will help you with so many things. Just say a little whisper, and it will do what you need." And Titari handed the wand to Willow.

"Thank you, Titari," Willow said excitedly. "I will keep it with me always. I can't wait to show the other fairies the gift you gave me and the beautiful tree you made so happy. I have to go find the others. It was very nice meeting you, Titari, and I hope to see you again soon." And Willow went off to find the others.

Isabelle and Titari stayed and looked at the tree and her brand new leaves for a bit before they started again through the woods. "This has been a really good day," Isabelle told Titari. "That tree is so proud of her leaves. And she did look different from any other. I'm glad things are different here. It makes the world so colorful. Can you imagine if all the animals looked the same? You wouldn't be able to tell a bear from a kitty. And if all the plants looked the same, you couldn't tell a rose from a lily. And if everyone looked the same, I wouldn't know which fairy I was talking to! You're right. Different is good."

Part Twelve

Blade Has a Gift to Give

"Let's go this way for a while," said Isabelle. "And see who we run into."

"Oh, don't say run into," Titari said. "I'm still trying to get over the bump I got from Bumble." And they both laughed as they went along through the woods. "It must be getting on in the day," Isabelle told Titari. "And we will have to start for the cottage soon."

"I am starting to understand why the fairies love to live here," Titari said. "This is such a wonderful place. The sounds of the animals and the smell of the flowers are so nice."

After walking for a while, Titari saw a line of ants, and they stopped to watch them make their way across a log. "It's wonderful how everything works together here," Titari said. "I hope I can spend a lot of time here in the woods."

"You can come as often as you like," Isabelle told her. "You have many friends here." Titari smiled. Her heart warmed with the thought of having friends. She was all by herself on the moon.

They had just started on their way again when Feather flew up. "I am so glad I found you," Feather told them. "I have been looking for you both."

"Is there anything wrong?" Isabelle asked. "No. Nothing is wrong, but could you please come with me? I have something to show you." Isabelle and Titari followed Feather back through the woods wondering why Feather needed them. If nothing was wrong, what could be so important?

They came to a small clearing in the woods, and all the fairies were gathered there. "They're here," yelled Hunny. "They made it," yelled Bunny as they flew up to meet them. "We are so glad that Feather found you," Petal told them as they reached the others. "We have all gathered here waiting for you because we want to talk to Titari."

"To me?" Titari asked. "Did I do something wrong?"

"Oh no, you done nothing wrong," said Dew Drop. "We just have a question to ask you."

"And we want you both to stay for a party," Maze added.

"We would love to stay for your party," Isabelle said. "What is the party for?"

"It's for our new friend," said Hopper. "To welcome her and thank her for the gifts she gave us."

"Yes," said Willow. "We are all very thankful to have such a kind and helpful new friend."

"Wow," said Titari. "I don't know what to say? Thank you, all of you. But you didn't have to go to any trouble for me."

"It was no trouble," Bumble told her. "And we wanted to welcome you to the woods the right way."

"Some of us have been following you both through the woods and listening to you talk," Feather told them. "And we have a question to ask Titari before we do anything else."

"What is it you want to know?" Titari asked. "Well," said Dew Drop, "we have been listening to you talk about how you love the woods."

"Yes, I do," said Titari. "It is so beautiful here."

"And we were wondering," said Hunny. "Yes, we were wondering," said Bunny. "What is it?" asked Isabelle. "I'm on my toes with excitement. Just ask her."

"We were wondering," came another voice from behind the fairies, "if you would like to stay here and live in the woods with us?"

"It's Blade," said Isabelle to Titari. "I am very pleased to meet you, Titari," said Blade. "I have heard a lot about you. I am Blade, and I make everything the fairies need."

"I'm glad to meet you, Blade," Titari answered. "Well," asked Blade, "what do you think?"

"About what?" Titari asked. "About living here in the woods with us," answered Blade.

Titari didn't know what to say. She was so excited to have all these new friends that want her to stay in the woods. "But where will I live here?" asked Titari. "I don't have a home or anything to even put in one."

"We have that all taken care of," said Willow. "Please follow us." And they all walked over to the tree with the star leaves. "Oh, Titari, look," said Isabelle. And right up in the middle of the star tree was a small house just the right size for Titari. And it was fully furnished with everything she would need, even some new clothes.

"I don't know what to say," Titari said. "Just say yes," said Willow. Titari looked at Isabelle, and Isabelle nodded her head. "Well," said Titari. "yes! I would love to stay and live here in the woods with all my new friends! I can't believe you all did this just for me."

"We thought," said Maze, "since you were from the moon that the star tree was the best place for you to live."

"Yes," said Hopper. "That way you won't get homesick."

"It's beautiful," Titari said with a tear in her eye. "And I won't get homesick cause I am home! Home by all my wonderful new friends!"

"We do have one more question for you, Titari, if you don't mind?" asked Maze. "You gave all of us a gift, and with it, you said to say a little whisper. But you never said what to whisper."

"I didn't, did I?" asked Titari. "I am sorry. But first I would like to give Blade a gift, and then I will tell you all what to whisper."

"A gift for me?" said Blade. "I am usually the one giving things to the others."

"This is a special gift from me," said Titari, and she reached in her pouch and pulled out a small, shining, heart-shaped stone. "This is the heart of the sun, and it is just for you." And she handed the stone to Blade. "But what do I do with it?" Blade asked. "Just hold it up high above your head, and say a little whisper. You will see."

Blade held the stone up high and looked at Titari. She went up and whispered in his ear and smiled. Blade looked up at the stone and said a little whisper, and a light shot out of the stone straight up into the sky. And *boom,* fireworks exploded from the light and lit up the sky with a rainbow of colors! "Yeah!" everyone yelled with excitement. "Let the party begin!"

"But what about the rest of them?" asked Isabelle. "You haven't told them the whisper yet."

"Oh yes," said Titari. "To get your gifts to work, all you have to do is whisper, 'With all my heart!'"

And with that, the party started! Hunny and Bunny played music. Petal and Maze set up the food. Maze even grew some of the candy mushrooms for everyone! Blade took Titari to see everything in her new house, and everyone ate and danced and sang. They had so much fun, and everyone was happy. But Titari was the happiest of them all.

After a few hours of dancing, they all sat down to talk about their first meeting Titari. They talked about how different they thought she was and how they realized that she may look different, but she's still a good friend. Titari gave Isabelle a big hug. "Thank you, Isabelle," she told her. "For what?" asked Isabelle. "For wishing on the star that brought me here. I promise I will come visit you often, and I will never forget the special gift that you gave me—friendship!"

Part Thirteen

From a Child to a Fairy

As I said in the front of this book, it is written for all those who call me Nana. Each fairy in this story is made after one of my grandchildren. And even Isabelle and Titari have a special place in my heart. So I would like to take the time now to explain which is who and why.

Feather is for Precious. I chose Feather, the keeper of the birds, because of the wings. For she too flies above us with the wings of an angel in heaven.

Dew Drop is for Cassie. I chose Dew Drop, the keeper of the water and water creatures, because every year on her birthday, she wants to go down to the creek and catch crawfish with her Papaw.

Petal is for Jasmine. I chose Petal, the keeper of the flowers, because of how she has blossomed from a shy little girl to a beautiful young lady.

Hopper is for Scotty Jr. I chose Hopper, the keeper of all the creatures that go from water to land, because of how much he loves lizards and turtles and such.

Maze is for Lexi. I chose Maze, the keeper of all plants in the woods, because of her love of decorating and making sure that everything has a special place. And every place has something special.

Hunny is for Hailie. I chose Hunny, the keeper to the animals and twin to fairy Bunny, because she has such a big heart and a love for everything.

Bunny is for Bayli. I chose Bunny, also keeper to the animals and twin to fairy Hunny, because of her love for giraffes and squirrels.

But you must also know that I made Hailie and Bayli twins because they are two peas in a pod!

Bumble is for Nick. I chose Bumble, the keeper to all the bugs because, well, simply because he is and always will be Nana's little bug!

Willow is for Saydee. I chose Willow, the keeper to all the trees, because of her love for the outdoors.

Blade is for Rex. I chose Blade, fairy tinker and maker of all fairy things needed, because of his love of making things for others.

Isabelle was named after my grandmother, Mary Isabelle. The name, like her, has always been special to me.

The animals at the cottage, May, Burke, Micah, Jersey, and Nanny, were just names that I thought fit for those friends.

And last but not least, the moon sprite that won everyone's friendship.

Titari is for my two little girls at home, well, my dogs. Named after the Egyptian queens—Nefertiti and Nefertari. They are simply called Ti and Tari.

I hope you enjoyed reading this story as much as I have writing it. And to all those who call me Nana, I would like you to know that Nana loves you with all my heart!

About the Author

Linda Acton lives in Indiana with the man of her dreams, John, six children, twelve grandchildren, and one great-grandchild. She loves to visit family and travels often to see those that don't live close. In her spare time, when not writing, she loves to make jewelry, cook, and care for their many pets. Her grandchildren are the most important people in her heart, and she tries to spoil them as much as possible. She is not a Cadillac type of person instead she prefers a minivan so she can fit as many grandchildren as possible. One of her favorite things is the family zoo trip that they try to do once a year. Her friends and family say she is the kindest, most loving person you could meet. Linda has a love for life and strong belief in the fairy world. Her imagination is as big as her heart, and she always finds the beauty in life.

JUL 19 2019

9 781645 440000